GW00891115

Lorna and th
Loch Ness Monster

Published by New Generation Publishing in 2019

www.newgeneration-publishing.com

New Generation Publishing

Acknowledgements

I am indebted to Historic Environment Scotland in Edinburgh for allowing me to use Urquhart Castle as the venue for my story about Lorna. They also kindly provided images of this former royal castle that played a vital part in the history of Scotland. One of which can be seen on the back of the book.

My sincere thanks to Jess Hawksworth for her enchanting illustrations, particularly of our pretty female monster, 'Heather'. Jess has captured her warm personality and we plan to collaborate on further children's stories in the future.

I would also just like to say here that 'Nessie' or 'Heather', as we now know she prefers to be called, must exist because Lorna has met her!

Lorna and the Loch Ness Monster

Eight-year-old Lorna, her Mum and Dad and her brother, Luke, went to Loch Ness for a short holiday. Luke was three years older than Lorna and he liked to tease her.

Loch Ness was a very long way from where they lived in Manchester, but their dad had told them there was a ruined castle near the campsite where they were staying, and Lorna was excited as she loved exploring castles.

But she was also a little scared. In the car, while they were driving up, Luke had said there was a huge monster in Loch Ness that would eat her up if she went in the water.

'It can't get me if we're in a boat though, can it?' Lorna asked. 'I won't be in the water then, will I?'

'No,' said Luke. 'But it'll know you're on the boat and might tip it over. Then it can eat you up!'

Her mum laughed when Lorna told her what Luke had said. 'Well, big brothers like scaring little sisters. Your Uncle David did the same with me when I was your age. Don't you take any notice and, anyway, the Loch Ness monster is just a story that someone made up…it doesn't really exist.' But she told Luke off for frightening Lorna anyway.

'I was just joking,' Luke said. 'I know the monster isn't really real.'

Well, Lorna thought about that. If the monster didn't exist, how did everyone know about it? But just in case it did, she decided to stay on land where she would be safe. The monster couldn't get her if she stayed out of the water!

When they arrived at the campsite, they drove up to a huge silver caravan.

'This is ours,' said Dad. 'Come on, let's get unpacked and then we can go and have a look around.' Lorna thought the caravan looked enormous!

Later, after tea in the campsite café, Dad asked if they would like a boat ride around the loch. Mum and Luke said, 'Yes!' But Lorna shook her head and asked if they could try archery instead. They all agreed that would be fun, so Dad said the boat ride could wait until the next day.

But, the next morning, when Dad suggested the boat ride again. Lorna shook her head and asked if they could go cycling and, as everyone liked riding bikes, that was what they did.

The following day, again Dad suggested the boat ride. Mum and Luke wanted to go, but Lorna asked if they could visit the old castle.

'Well, I suppose I did promise her,' Dad said.

'Oh, but castles are boring,' said Luke, 'especially the ruined ones.'

'Tomorrow we'll go on the boat. I promise,' said Dad. But, they all enjoyed the wonderful tour around the castle ruins, even Luke.

They went up into the tower where they could look across the loch, watched a film about the history of the castle, and saw a display showing what it would have looked like when people actually lived there. There were lots of old weapons, which Luke enjoyed looking at, and running around the walls was great fun.

But Lorna wasn't interested in weapons and, while Luke was pointing out some special swords to their parents, Lorna ran over to one of the outside walls and clambered up to walk along the top. Her family had not noticed she was no longer with them.

Hearing a strange cheeping sound above her, Lorna looked up to see a big bird with a wide wingspan and was not watching where she was going. Suddenly she slipped, and before anyone saw what had happened, she fell into a dark hole and slid for what seemed like ages.

Her shouts for help were muffled inside the tunnel, but soon it seemed to even out, like the bottom part of a slide in a playground, and she slid onto what appeared to be a pebbly beach inside a watery cave. She had lots of bruises and had scraped her knees and elbows, and one of the side pockets of her shorts was torn, but she was more worried and shocked than sore.

She looked up the tunnel to see if there was any way she could get back to her family. But no, it was too slippery, and she couldn't see anything to hold onto to help her climb back up. She didn't swim very well and the water in the cave looked too deep for her to paddle through it. What was she to do? She was very frightened. It would soon get dark outside and she knew her family would be worried, but how would they find her?

At the mouth of the cave the gentle ripples of the water grew into waves. Something was moving towards her under the surface. She looked for somewhere to hide, but there was nowhere!

A long head rose up from the water followed by a much longer neck and body. 'Hello,' said the monster. 'Wha' are yeh doing in mah cave?'

'I...I'm really...so...sorry, Mr Monster,' said Lorna nervously, and not a little shocked -

who knew monsters could talk? 'I just sort of slid in through that tunnel,' she said, pointing to the hole in the wall. 'Are you the Loch Ness Monster?'

'Well, aye, but I'm no a Mister...Ah'm a Miss Monster and Ah've heard folk call me Nessie, but I don't like tha' name. I like Fiona, and Heather, aye Heather. That's a bonny name. What's your name? Would you like to stay with me? You'd be very welcome as Ah get a wee bit lonely here on mah ain. I could bring yeh fish, freshwater shrimps and water weed tae eat every day, so yeh'd no be hungry.'

'Oh, yes. I'm sorry, my name is Lorna. And, thank you for asking, but I really need to get back to my family, they'll be worried about me. I just don't know how.' And she started crying.

'Och, please dinna cry, lassie. Dinna fret, Ah can take yeh back. All yeh need tae dae is climb up on mah neck. Look, Ah'll come up onto the beach tae make it easier for yeh tae get on, but Ah warn yeh, the water is very cold, and yeh must hang on tightly. Yeh'll get wet Ah'm afraid, but yeh'll no be in the water fer long. The jetty where I'll leave yeh is quite nearby.'

'Thank you, Heather.' Lorna wiped her tears away with the back of her hand. 'That's very good of you.'

As Heather waded out of the water and onto the beach, Lorna was amazed to see she had no feet. Instead she had what looked like the oars people use to row a boat, and she sort of waddled up on to the stones.

She was almost completely out of the water when she stopped, leaned forward and picked something up off the beach with her mouth. Lorna wondered if Heather had found something to eat.

Climbing up, Lorna wrapped her arms tightly around Heather's neck. 'I hope I'm not choking you,' she said.

Heather smiled and said, through almost closed lips, 'Nae, that's quite comfortable, thank yeh, and dinna worry, Ah'll no have tae take yeh under the water. We'll be on the surface all the time.'

On the way back, Lorna told Heather about her family and that they lived in Manchester but were there on holiday for a few days.

Keeping very close to the shoreline, and hidden by the trees and plants, Heather lowered her head and slid under the jetty leaving enough room to make sure Lorna didn't bump her own head on the wooden boards above them.

'Well, we've no been seen and Ah'm guessing that'll be your family up there wi' all those other people. Ah'd much rather they didnae know about me, if yeh dinna mind. But it's been very nice tae meet yeh and, if yeh visit this way again, please dinna ferget tae come and see me.'

'Oh, I will and thank you for all your help,' said Lorna.

'Afore yeh go, Lorna, I'd like tae gi' yeh a wee present,' said Heather. 'It's just a wee somethin' tae remember me by.' And, when she opened her mouth in a wide smile, Lorna saw something shiny wedged between two of Heather's teeth. It looked like a button.

'That's fer yeh, Lorna. Yeh can take it, and dinna worry, Ah promise Ah'll no bite.'

'But what is it?' asked Lorna, reaching up to take it. Holding the small brooch-shaped thing in the palm of her hand, she could see it was a circle, looking like a closed-up belt with a lion standing in the middle and some letters which Lorna could not read around the edge. She thought it was very unusual.

'Och, a long time ago, when Ah was just a wee thing, there were lots of battles around here, and men kept trying to take the castle from each other. Ah remember one man, who seemed tae be in charge, had this wee button torn off his shirt in a fight on the shore. Ah think Ah heard someone call him The Bruce. Anyway, he didnae seem to notice it had gone, so when they went away, Ah took it into mah cave and kept it with some other shiny things Ah'd found. But now I'd like yeh tae have it because yeh're mah new pal.'

'Thank you, Heather. I will keep it forever and I won't ever forget you.' Lorna put the button in the side pocket of her shorts – the one that wasn't torn.

'Yeh'd better go. Ah can see yer family are worried,' said Heather.

'But, what do I say about how I got out of the cave and onto the jetty?' Lorna had no idea how to explain it without telling her family about Heather.

'When they ask, just say yeh waded through the water holding on tae the reeds on the bank until yeh got to the jetty. They'll all believe yeh because they'll no be able to think of any other explanation and yeh're certainly wet enough, so yeh'd better go and get dry and warm now. Goodbye, Lorna. It was lovely to meet yeh.'

'Goodbye…Heather. It was lovely to meet you too, and thank you so much for helping me, and for my gift.'

Heather, the Loch Ness Monster smiled, and, with a wave of her tail, she swam away out of sight as Lorna clambered up onto the jetty and began running up the path. 'Mum! Dad!' she shouted. They turned and rushed down the path to meet her, but Luke got to her first and gave her a hug.

'Hi Sis,' he grinned. 'Glad you're OK but what happened to you?'

'The monster saved me,' she said.

'Yeah. Whatever!' Luke chuckled. 'You know monsters don't exist.'

'Yes. I know. I'm just joking,' Lorna smiled, and she patted the side pocket of her shorts.

'Dad, can we go for a boat ride on the loch tomorrow, please?' asked Lorna.

Lightning Source UK Ltd.
Milton Keynes UK
UKHW051255190920
370158UK00005B/43